a Gramma Rae story
illustrated by
Phyllis Dorriety Mignard

Desert Rose Publishing
Las Vegas, Nevada

Printed in Singapore

Text Copyright © 1990 by Della Rae Clark

Illustrations Copyright © 1992 by Phyllis Dorriety Mignard

All rights reserved. No part of this publication may be reproduced or transmitted in any form or by any means, electronic or mechanical, including photocopy, recording or any information storage and retrieval system without written permission from the publisher, except for the inclusion of brief quotations in a review.

Publisher's Cataloging In Publications Data
Clark, Della Rae
Quiet One
63 p.   27 cm.
ISBN 0-9631252-0-6
1. Indians of North America — Fiction
2. Nature — Fiction
I. Title
LCC Card Number 92-70830

To all my sweethearts
that I know and love —
and to those I'm about to meet.
— Gramma Rae

The Baby

Blue Jay hopped nervously from limb to limb in the big pine tree, but his usually noisy voice was strangely still. His worried black eyes flicked from Princess Windsong to her tiny newborn son on a soft carpet of boughs and moss beneath the tree. Why didn't the baby cry? Didn't all babies cry when they were born? Could it be that the breath of life had not entered him?

Strong Eagle, pacing back and forth nearby, was also waiting to hear the sound of crying to know that his beloved wife had given birth to their child. Suddenly, in a flash of blue feathers, Blue Jay was circling above Strong Eagle, calling loudly for him to hurry to his wife.

What was wrong? Strong Eagle had heard no cry! With his heart pounding in his chest as if it would burst, he charged through the bushes like a wild buffalo.

The sun sparkled with joy as it shone down on the family in the deep forest. With a beautiful smile, the young mother handed her husband their tiny son wrapped in velvety deerskin.

"Our son is healthy and strong like his father," Princess Windsong said with music in her voice, "but he came so

peacefully and with such silence that I know he is different from other babies."

Strong Eagle looked at his wife for a long moment, then again at the boy baby whose wide-open eyes seemed to be searching his father's face. "Then his name will be Quiet One," he announced.

With Princess Windsong holding onto his arm, Strong Eagle carried his son back to their village. All the people came to meet them, to look at and touch this baby who would one day become their chief. Quiet One still had his eyes wide open, exploring this new world he had just entered, and everyone saw that he was indeed different from all other babies in their tribe.

Leaving his wife at their teepee, Strong Eagle went to her father's teepee and stepped inside the flap, proudly holding out his son. "Meet your grandfather," Strong Eagle said gently to the baby. "He is Wise Owl, chief of our people."

Sitting calmly on a buffalo robe with his legs folded in front of him, Chief Wise Owl reached out to take the baby from Strong Eagle's arms. His eyes brightened as they examined his new grandson.

Strong Eagle looked into Chief Wise Owl's face with its deep lines and knew the wisdom in his eyes and the love in his heart. "Chief of my people," Strong Eagle said, "you have been as a father to me ever since my own father was killed on Rattlesnake Pass, and I am proud to have your daughter for my wife. I ask you now to help us guide the feet of our son along whatever trail the Great Spirit has marked for him to travel. His name will be Quiet One."

"Yes," Wise Owl answered, "I shall help him walk with the Great Spirit." The wise old chief stood, lifted the baby toward the sky and silently prayed to the Great Spirit to bless this small one with strength of body and peace of heart and mind.

Then Wise Owl's eyes seemed to look far beyond the village as he went on, "Even when she was a baby, there was music in my daughter's voice. It was like a breeze whispering in the pine trees, and I wanted her spirit to be free as the air. So after talking to the Great Spirit, her name was called Windsong. Strong Eagle, your father had reasons for naming you after a powerful bird, and you, in turn, have reasons for naming your son Quiet One."

"To this name I add my blessings and now tell you what the Great Spirit told me about your son. We must all know that Quiet One is most unusual. He was born with a special love for the world, with special purpose and with knowledge to teach his people many things. Do not expect him to live life as you do, for he will have greater understanding of all things."

Strong Eagle held his tiny son close to his chest as he left Wise Owl and walked toward his teepee. He stopped outside the flap and listened to the autumn song his wife was singing:

*See the colorful autumn leaves
Dancing with the brisk and swirling wind.
Come, they beckon, join us in the celebration
Of the season's end.*

Smiling at the beauty of her song, he stepped inside and put Quiet One in his mother's arms. "I think he is hungry," he said. The baby nuzzled his mother's breast and made smacking sounds. "See, he doesn't cry even when he is hungry," she murmured.

Strong Eagle sat on the fur bed with his beloved wife and put his arms protectively around her and the nursing baby, holding them close. In his happiness at the birth of his fine son, he had almost forgotten that this was autumn, the time when the whole village was preparing to move to their winter lodges in the lower valleys. He had almost forgotten the fear his people felt, knowing they must cross the horrible Rattlesnake Pass again.

Rattlesnake Pass

Rattlesnake Pass got its name from the deadly rattlesnake because the trail was winding and crawled around the mountain like a snake. Hacked and chipped out of the rocky cliffs by an ancient tribe of people, the narrow trail allowed only one at a time. But, most of all, it was very, very dangerous.

Crossing the pass itself was not a long journey, but because of the danger and the slow, crawling pace required, it took from sunup to sundown. Getting down to the valleys was a long trek because this mountain meadowland was surrounded by high, rocky cliffs called crags.

There was no other way to get from the high mountain country, where they spent their summers each year, down to the lower valleys where there was less snow in the winters. High in these Rocky Mountains which the Indians called home, the game was plentiful and life was joyous during the summer, but winter brought deep snows and much cold. They had to go to the lower valleys or they would die.

The Indians used their ponies to help them cross Rattlesnake Pass but they did not ride them. Instead, the ponies were packed with their belongings and then tied head to tail. Rawhide ropes were tied around the neck, under the chin and over the nose of each pony and then tied very close to the tail of another pony. All the ponies tied together in this way were called a pack string.

The ponies were tied close together so they couldn't look around or throw their heads up. If they did, it would throw them off balance. They could lose their footing and fall to certain death. The Indians tied a special knot in each pony's tail with rawhide rope. If one pony should slip, stumble, or fall over the cliff, the knot would free itself from the tail it was tied to.

All the Indians walked single file. Babies were carried on their mothers' backs. The small children had short rawhide ropes tied around their waists with the other end tied to the father or mother in front of them.

The half-way mark of Rattlesnake Pass was called Killem Point, where it looked as if the trail just dropped off the cliff. The Indians had to make a sharp turn with their bodies leaning against the rocks to get around it, and the ponies had to do the same. Many Indians and ponies lost their lives here, and that is why it was called Killem Point.

After they got around the point, they started down, which was more difficult than going up. Climbing was hard and tiring and slow, but going down was even more difficult because it was steep and the tiny pebbles shifted under their feet. If they slipped, they fell on their bottoms and started sliding until they were stopped by the one in front of them.

The men were placed between every two or three women, and just the strongest of the men led the ponies.

The whole journey over Rattlesnake Pass was done in complete silence. No child cried, no voice was heard, no pony grunted. Even the air was still. Only when they reached Killem Point could they hear the Whispering Wind. From where it came no one knew, but it was always there. Many believed it was the spirits of those who had lost their lives at the point. Many pretended the Whispering Wind was not there, and they would not listen or even talk about it. The crossing of Rattlesnake Pass was indeed a treacherous journey.

The Journey

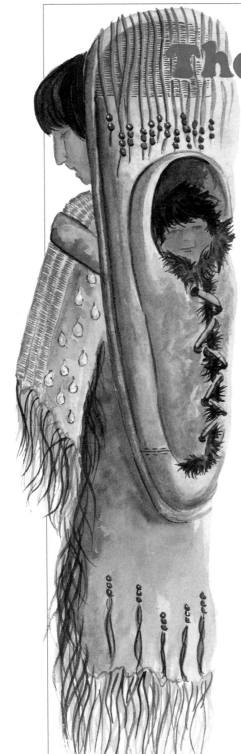

Indian summer was over, and the village was preparing for the journey to the lower valleys. When the day for the journey arrived, everyone in the village was up before the sun. All the ponies were packed with teepees, food, and other belongings. Everyone was busy getting ready, but no one was talking. The early morning air was crisp and still, and you could feel the silence as each one took his place to start up the trail.

Strong Eagle led the ponies because he was the biggest and strongest of all the Indians. Princess Windsong walked in front of Strong Eagle with Quiet One on her back. Quiet One was enjoying the whole thing. He was snug and warm, and he could watch his father leading the ponies.

The sun was halfway across the sky as they approached Killem Point. Everyone was tired from the steep climb, but there was no sound. Strong Eagle wondered if anyone could hear the pounding of his heart as he watched his wife and son near Killem Point. Very slowly Princess Windsong pressed her shoulder against the mountain and, one step at a time, with her small hands clinging to the cliff, she made the sharp turn. For just a moment she was out of the sight of Strong Eagle, and his thoughts were so on his family that he forgot about the ponies. He felt a sudden jerk just as he made the sharp turn and saw them. The rawhide rope jerked his arm high in the air as the pony reared off its front feet. He grabbed the rope with both hands as his feet went flying off the trail. Strong Eagle was hanging over the cliff!

The pony's eyes were wild with terror as he half-sat and half-stood with his quivering body leaning into the mountain. The rope was cutting Strong Eagle's hands as he held on tightly. He tried desperately to get a footing in the soft shale rock at the edge of the cliff. He tried time and time again until his arms were aching and his hands were bleeding. The pony's head was still held high with such fright that it couldn't move. Strong Eagle's feet were bleeding through his moccasins as he dug them into the rocks. Princess Windsong buried her face in her hands. She could not watch.

Suddenly the pony's head jerked into the mountain, and Strong Eagle found himself flat against the cliff with his burning feet firmly on the trail. He closed his eyes as his head and body melted into the rocks of the mountain. His arms were still pulled high above his head by the terrified, quivering pony. Strong Eagle turned to the pony, keeping the rope very tight, and reached out and touched the pony's nose, rubbing it gently.

The pony started to relax his neck and lowered his head to Strong Eagle's chest. Strong Eagle put one arm around the pony's neck and stroked him firmly, urging him to get to his feet. The pony understood and very carefully stood up. Strong Eagle laid his forehead against the pony's forehead and silently thanked him for saving his life.

Strong Eagle turned to Princess Windsong and saw tears running down her face like rivers. Strong Eagle then looked down over the cliff where so many had lost their lives. Horse Creek that flowed between the high mountains looked like a small, shimmering silver cord. It was so far down! He closed his eyes again and thanked the Great Spirit that he wasn't lying at the bottom.

Strong Eagle reached out and rubbed the pony's nose again, then led the pack string around Killem Point. Princess Windsong continued down the trail singing her song of thankfulness:

My heart soars with happiness
As on wings far above,
For the Great Spirit once again has
Touched us,
With his ever present love.

Grandfather

Eight journeys had been made over Rattlesnake Pass, and Quiet One had walked behind his mother during the last six. He did not fear the journey over the pass as the rest of the people in the village did. He found all of life to be wonderful. He loved his beautiful mother, his strong father, and all the people in his village. He also deeply loved the forest and the animals that lived there, but most of all, he loved his Grandfather, Wise Owl, who told many wonderful stories and never grew tired of talking to him.

Early one morning, he ran to his Grandfather's teepee. As Quiet One went through the flap, Wise Owl smiled warmly and greeted his grandson with a big hug. He was sitting on a fur blanket with his legs crossed underneath him. Quiet One took the same position in front of him so he could look into his Grandfather's warm, bright eyes.

Quiet One asked, "Grandfather, do you know the Great Spirit, the one that you and all the rest talk about so much?"

Grandfather said, "Yes," looking curiously into the boy's eyes.

Quiet One continued, "Who is the Great Spirit? What is it and where is it?"

Grandfather smiled and said, "God is the Great Spirit. This Great Spirit created the whole universe — all the men, women and children, trees, flowers, every blade of grass, all the animals, the fish, the mountains, lakes, streams, the sun, the moon, and the stars. Everything you see, feel, or hear is the Great Spirit. The Great Spirit lives in everything that has form and in everything without form, like the wind, the rays of sunlight, the air you breathe. You cannot see the wind or the air, but it is there."

Quiet One thought for a moment and then asked, "Grandfather, can anyone talk to the Great Spirit?"

Grandfather's eyes shone as he replied, "Yes, you can talk to the Great Spirit silently, with your heart. Then, stop talking and listen, and the Great Spirit will talk to you. It is good to be in a place where it is peaceful and still. Close your eyes and think about the Great Spirit. Ask the Great Spirit anything. This may take a little practice, but be patient, my grandson. The Great Spirit will talk to you and give you understanding."

"Oh, thank you, Grandfather, for telling me this!" Quiet One jumped to his feet, gave his Grandfather a hug, and ran off into the forest.

The Butterfly

Quiet One's heart was so happy, for he understood everything his grandfather had told him. He also knew that this old man was very wise and always told him the truth. He could hardly wait to get to the forest and talk to the Great Spirit.

Quiet One went to his favorite place and sat down by his big pine tree. There was a small stream that ran near the tree, and he could sit under the tree and watch the fish swim between the rocks and hide in the moss. There were flowers and tall grass on the small hills on each side of the big pine tree. Quiet One looked all around and smiled to himself. He thought of how much he loved this special place. He felt very thankful that the Great Spirit had created all this.

Quiet One lay on his back, folded his arms over his heart, and closed his eyes. He talked to the Great Spirit silently and asked the Great Spirit to give him understanding of everything. Then he tried to make his mind be silent and listen to the Great Spirit talk to him.

As he was listening very hard, he felt a light flutter on his forehead. He opened his eyes and saw a large butterfly. The butterfly fluttered again, and Quiet One's eyes crossed as the butterfly rested on his nose. Then a tiny voice chimed, "Hello, my name is Monica."

Quiet One, still looking cross-eyed, thought, "Is this the Great Spirit? The Great Spirit sounds like a girl!"

Monica giggled and said, "Yes, I am of the Great Spirit and so are you. The Great Spirit is all, and all are the Great Spirit. You can see me, hear me, and talk to me because as I flew over you, I felt your love vibration."

"I know what love is, but what is 'vibration'?"

"Thoughts are vibrations," answered Monica. "For example, your mother may wonder where you are and want you to come to the teepee. She doesn't call you with her voice. She sends out thought vibrations. You feel her voice in your mind, not in your ears, and you go to her. Also, there are fear vibrations, like when you want to ride a pony but are afraid. The pony feels your fear, and it makes him afraid of you. So when you try to get on his back, he throws you off. If you have love vibrations for the pony, he feels this, too, and will let you jump on his back."

"Do you have vibrations, too?" asked Quiet One.

"Oh, yes," said Monica. "My whole life depends on vibrations. My vibrations tell me to drink only the sweet juices from the milkweed because the juice from the milkweed makes me taste very bad. The birds know that and do not try to eat me. Also, my vibrations tell me where to lay my eggs, how far to fly, and where to fly."

"But where do vibrations come from?" asked Quiet One.

"That's what I have been telling you," said Monica. "Everything you feel, see, or hear was given to you by the Great Spirit. All you need to do is stop, look, and listen with love in your heart, and you will understand everything. Speaking of vibrations, mine just told me I must leave now and find a place to sleep before dark. Good-bye, Quiet One."

"Good-bye, Monica, and...thank you," he replied softly.

Quiet One was feeling vibrations, too. He could feel his mother's thoughts and knew she was looking for him because it was almost dark. He ran all the way back to his village and was out of breath when he reached his teepee. He sat down and looked at his mother and father. They smiled at him, and he felt the love vibrations Monica had told him about. He sat silently all through the meal and thought about his wonderful day.

"What are you thinking so hard about, my son?" asked Strong Eagle.

Quiet One told his mother and father all about his wonderful day and his talk with Monica. Princess Windsong and Strong Eagle looked at each other with amazement in their eyes. Then Strong Eagle remembered what Wise Owl had told him when Quiet One was born. "Trust this child, for he will have greater understanding of all things."

Strong Eagle cleared his throat and said, "What did this butterfly Monica look like?"

"Oh," said Quiet One, "she was so beautiful! I have never seen one like her before. She was brown like the earth and had white clouds on both of her wings. Inside these clouds were earth-colored spots with smaller white clouds in the center of the spots. They looked like eyes on her wings."

"My son," said Strong Eagle, "you saw and talked with the Great Mother of a special family of butterflies. She is the most sacred of all the family."

Quiet One smiled and thought how wonderful it was that he had made friends with such a very special butterfly. He curled up on his fur bed and fell asleep.

Princess Windsong gently pushed back her son's hair from his forehead and in a soft voice sang:

> *Dream your dreams, my Quiet One. I know you*
> *Feel and see*
> *More love in the wind and more colors than were*
> *Ever shown to me.*
> *Dream your dreams and see visions of brave*
> *Ones holding high a light,*
> *So you can run your chosen path, in the*
> *Darkness of the night.*

The Deer

All summer, Quiet One went into the forest to talk to the Great Spirit. He listened to the birds and understood their beautiful songs. He watched the flowers grow and knew they were there to brighten up the forest and make the air smell good. But the Great Spirit told him they were also there because each bird, butterfly, bee, and other insect had special ones to feed upon, which they recognized by the color and smell of the flower. The Great Spirit provides food and water not only for man but for all living things.

Quiet One loved and respected all the Great Spirit's creations. He would sit under the big pine tree and watch the squirrels eat pine nuts. The squirrels loved him, too.

One day, Quiet One was lying on his stomach watching the fish in the stream. He put his hand in the water, and the fish nibbled at his fingers. They, too, had no fear of him. While playing with the fish, he looked up and saw a baby deer walking toward the stream. The fawn saw Quiet One and paused for a moment. The little deer just twitched his ears, then came to the edge of the stream and started drinking. Quiet One was very still and thought how nice it was that this young deer wasn't afraid of him. The fawn stopped drinking and looked up at him.

Quiet One smiled, and to his surprise, the little deer jumped in the stream, crossed over, and walked right up to him. He put his wet cold nose on Quiet One's cheek and said, "Hello, my name is Gobi."

Quiet One was so happy! He had never had a deer come near him, much less talk to him. He patted the fawn's back and said, "Hello, my name is Quiet One."

"I know," said Gobi. "Everyone in the forest knows you. They know you love and understand each one of us."

"Everyone?" asked Quiet One.

"Oh, yes," said Gobi, "when you come into the forest everyone knows there is just love in your heart."

Quiet One's head dropped down, and he felt very sad.

"What is the matter? Why do you look so sad?" Gobi asked.

Quiet One raised his head and looked at Gobi. "It makes me sad because we hunt you for food and clothing. You are so beautiful and you are of the Great Spirit also. Why should you be created just to be hunted?"

"Oh, please don't think that," Gobi said softly. "We were created for many other reasons, too. We feed upon the grass of the forest so it doesn't grow so tall. Tall dry grass is the main cause of forest fires when the thunder and lightening come. We keep the forest very clean by eating the grass and weeds. If the Indians didn't hunt us, our numbers would grow so large that there wouldn't be enough grass and many of us would die of starvation."

Quiet One hugged the little deer's neck. "Thank you, Gobi, for giving me understanding of the way you live."

Gobi nuzzled his arm and said, "Now I must go."

"Will I see you again?"

"Of course, Quiet One. All you have to do is think about me, and I will be here." With that, Gobi crossed the stream and disappeared into the forest.

Quiet One slowly walked through the forest with a song in his heart about the excitement of learning:

Run toward each new day
Knowing that it will bring
The voice of a teacher
Whose name shall be
Summer, Autumn,
Winter, Spring.

The Whispering Wind

Summer was over and Quiet One was helping Strong Eagle pack the ponies to move down to the lower camp. This would be Quiet One's tenth journey over Rattlesnake Pass. He watched his people prepare for the journey with dread in their faces. He smiled at each one, sending his love vibrations to them, hoping they would not hold this terrible fear in their hearts.

On the trail to Rattlesnake Pass, the pack string moved very slowly. The climb was steep and they needed many rest stops. As they neared Killem Point, again the silence was so deep that Quiet One could hear the Whispering Wind.

He had a strange feeling as he came closer to Killem Point that the Whispering Wind was almost alive with meaning. He so much wanted to stop and listen, for he knew the wind with its urgent whispering sound had some kind of message for him.

As he reached Killem Point, he could not stop, but he tried very hard to listen. He could not cause any danger to the rest of his people, so he carefully moved around Killem Point and the Whispering Wind faded as he started down the trail.

Quiet One could not get the Whispering Wind off his mind. "I must come back by myself and stop and listen. I know the Whispering Wind is trying to talk to me. I just have to know!"

When they reached the lower camp, Quiet One worked very hard helping his father set up their teepee and his mother unpack. Then he started gathering firewood. He gathered a great deal until he had it stacked around the teepee as high as he could reach.

Strong Eagle walked up beside Quiet One and put his hand on his shoulder, "My son, you do not have to bring the whole forest to our teepee in one day."

Quiet One said, "Yes, I know, Father, but I will be going on a short journey, and I want Mother to have enough firewood."

"Where are you going, my son?"

"Father, I must go to the Whispering Wind at Killem Point."

Strong Eagle looked into his son's eyes and did not question his reason for going. "When are you leaving, my son?"

"Before the sun rises, I will be gone," answered Quiet One.

Strong Eagle pulled his son to his chest. No further words were needed. They both understood.

Before the sun was up, Quiet One took a small fur blanket and some dried deer meat, rolled them up, and tied them with a rawhide string. He looped them over his shoulder and headed for Rattlesnake Pass, Killem Point, and the Whispering Wind.

Quiet One had seen the sun rise three times before he started up the trail for Rattlesnake Pass. He was enjoying the journey, watching animals of the forest hurry to prepare their food and shelter for the winter. Feeling the wind getting much colder, he took the fur blanket off his shoulder and unrolled it. He took the dried deer meat, rolled it in some loose bark, and tied it to his waist. Then he wrapped the fur blanket around his shoulders and tied it under his chin. Both hands had to be free in order for him to make the steep climb. The wind grew stronger and colder as he reached Killem Point.

The sound of the wind changed — now it was whispering. Quiet One sat down and pulled the fur blanket tightly around himself. With his eyes closed, he talked to the Great Spirit and listened very hard to the Whispering Wind. Quiet One sat all through the night. He tried harder and harder to hear what the Whispering Wind was saying, but he could not understand. He felt discouraged, and he was so cold.

Then he remembered what his grandfather had told him, "Do not grab at your silence. Just let go of all your thoughts and let it come like a small feather drifting down from the sky. When you grab at the small feather, it moves away. Just be still, open your hand, and it will rest gently in your palm." Quiet One thought of the small feather and felt peaceful.

The morning sun peeked over the mountains, and its warmth felt good on his face. As he was enjoying this warmth, he had a wonderful feeling and then heard, "GOOOO THEEEE OTHERRRR WAYYYY." Yes, Quiet One finally understood what the Whispering Wind was saying: "Go the other way."

Quiet One stood and looked far below, then he looked up at the cliffs above his head and to each side of him. He thought, "Go the other way?" Aloud he said, "What other way? I am no bird, I can't fly to the top of the cliffs. I am no snake, I can't crawl down the cliff. Tell me, Whispering Wind, what other way?" But the Whispering Wind said no more.

Quiet One sat down. He knew the message the Whispering Wind had given him. There was another way to get to the lower camp besides Rattlesnake Pass and Killem Point. As he was still, with his eyes closed, he began to see a picture in his mind. First, he saw a brilliant golden light. Then, surrounding the golden light were pine trees with a huge rock in front of the light. Finally, the light faded, and he saw no more.

Quiet One stood up and looked all around again for a long time, but he saw no other way. He looked up at the sky and saw that it had started snowing, so he started down the trail. He loved the snow and loved to watch it fall gently from the sky — like the small white feathers in his silence. But soon it was coming down very heavily and it became difficult to see the trail. The fur blanket across his back was white now instead of black. He wished he had worn his fur boots because his feet were getting cold. He started running to warm them, but the snow was coming down so hard that

he couldn't see. He was glad he was off Rattlesnake Pass and on a wide part of the trail.

The snow came down harder and harder, heavier and heavier, until Quiet One had to stop running because he could no longer see any part of the trail. Through the trees, he saw some deer and thought of Gobi. No sooner had he thought of his friend than Gobi was there, standing right beside him!

"Come," said Gobi, "I will take you to the caves."

Quiet One had seen the caves many times from the trail but never had been inside them. Gobi led him up the winding trail. When they reached the caves, it was dark and snowing even harder.

Gobi said, "You will be safe here."

"Thank you, Gobi."

Gobi nuzzled Quiet One's chest with his head and said, "Now I must go and join the rest of my family." Then the deer turned and darted off into the night.

The Bear

Quiet One got down on his hands and knees and crawled inside the cave. It was very, very dark and he couldn't see a thing. But he could smell, and what he was smelling was a bear! He stopped for a moment and listened. He heard a grunt, then he heard something breathing. He knew that bears slept all winter in the caves, but he didn't know how soundly. Slowly, Quiet One sat down with his cold, wet feet folded under him and pulled his blanket tightly around himself. As hard as he tried, he could not get warm. The bear grunted again, and Quiet One knew it was very close. He reached out his hand to see how close. He couldn't touch the bear but could feel the warmth of its body.

He slowly inched his way toward the sleeping bear until he touched the warm fur with his fingertips. Carefully, he stretched his leg toward the warmth and put one cold foot under the bear, and then the other foot. "Oh, how warm this bear is!" thought Quiet One. The cold was leaving his feet. He thanked the Great Spirit for this wonderful foot warmer and sent love vibrations to the bear. He lay down on his back and fell asleep.

Quiet One was aroused by a heavy thud on top of his head — a huge paw was covering his face. He lay very still. Then he realized that his whole body was snuggled next to the bear. The bear was warm, but, oh, he smelled so awful!

He wanted to move away, but he surely did not want to awaken the bear, for he had heard that bears were very grumpy if anyone or anything disturbed their winter's sleep.

Very carefully, Quiet One lifted the huge paw with its long claws off his face and slowly wormed away from the bear. As gently as he could, he put the paw down and sat up. He looked at the sleeping bear and smiled, silently thanking him for sharing his bed.

Quiet One crawled to the entrance of the cave and looked out. Everything was white and so beautiful. What a wonderful picture the Great Spirit had painted! There wasn't an animal in sight. Nothing was moving, only the soft snow was gently falling. Quiet One took a deep breath and smelled the clean air. He sat down to look at the undisturbed peacefulness of this beautiful white forest. He unrolled the bark and ate his breakfast of dried meat. He felt as peaceful as the snowflakes gently drifting to the ground. In his memory, he heard his mother's song of faith:

> *How sweet and gentle is the Great Spirit*
> *Of love and peace.*
> *It falls upon me so softly in a coat of*
> *Pure white fleece.*
> *What warmth in just knowing its presence*
> *Within me abides.*
> *I can run free with the wind from the light*
> *That glows inside.*

Quiet One finished his meal, then he closed his eyes and thanked the Great Spirit for guidance. As he thanked the Great Spirit, the brilliant golden light, the pine trees, and the big rock filled his mind. It was the same vision he had seen at Killem Point. Then he heard again in his mind the Whispering Wind telling him, "Go the other way." Quiet One knew there was another way for his people to get to the lower camp besides Rattlesnake Pass and Killem Point, and he knew he would find it. He jumped to his feet and ran down the trail.

When Quiet One reached his teepee, he told his mother and father everything. They listened with great interest. "I know there is another way," he cried, "and I will find it!"

Strong Eagle said, "Yes, I know you will, too, and when we return to our summer camp in the spring, you will join the Indian brothers to find the herd of wild ponies. You must have a pony to help you search these mountains."

Quiet One's eyes grew large. "My very own pony? How wonderful!"

The Planting

Winter seemed to be so very long for Quiet One. His thoughts were on the pony and on finding another way for his people to cross the mountains. Every time he closed his eyes and was silent, he saw the brilliant golden light, the pine trees, and the big rock. Grandfather had told him that the Great Spirit had given him this vision. He knew that when he found the golden light he would find the other way.

When at last winter was over and the snow had melted, Quiet One helped everyone take down their teepees and pack the ponies. He had such great excitement in his heart. Everyone in the village was happy, too. Maybe this was the last trip they would have to make over Rattlesnake Pass.

As they journeyed up the trail, they passed the caves and Quiet One looked up, wondering if the bear were still sleeping. He pointed to the cave where he had spent the night and turned to look at Princess Windsong. She smiled and nodded her head. She knew what her son was saying.

Quiet One could see Killem Point from the lower trail. He looked for the golden light, but saw nothing. Strong Eagle put his hand firmly on his son's shoulder. Quiet One didn't turn around, but he knew what his father was telling him. "Keep your mind on the trail. This is not the time to search for the golden light," was what his father said without words.

As they continued up the trail, Quiet One wondered if the Whispering Wind at Killem Point would tell him where to start looking for the golden light. He approached Killem

Point and the Whispering Wind with high hopes, but the wind was silent.

Everyone was happy to be back in the high mountains where the sun had warmed the earth and the flowers were starting to bloom. The ground was perfect for planting. While setting up their teepees, they sang together from the joy in their hearts:

> *Let us plant the seeds, my people,*
> *To till the body, mind, and spirit.*
> *Stretch out your arms and welcome*
> *The earth and all that's in it.*
>
> *Touch the wind that flows in your hair*
> *And breathe the birds' sweet song.*
> *Drink deep of love, hope, and happiness*
> *For to the Great Spirit we all belong.*

No one was in a hurry — no one except Quiet One. He worked very hard from sunup to sundown. Strong Eagle and Princess Windsong watched their son working so hard, but said nothing. They knew what was on his mind. In the evening while they were eating their meal, Quiet One asked his father, "When will we leave to find the ponies?"

"As soon as the corn is planted," answered Strong Eagle.

Quiet One said, "I will have ours planted tomorrow!"

"I am sure you could have ours planted tomorrow, my son, but remember, we do not go alone to find the ponies. All the Indian brothers will go, and they may not have their corn planted that quickly."

Quiet One smiled and nodded his head slightly, looking at his father. Strong Eagle smiled back. Quiet One got up and gave his bowl to his mother. He kissed her on the cheek. "I am going to sleep under the stars tonight," he said.

Princess Windsong touched his shoulder, "Sleep well, my son."

Quiet One walked outside the camp to the small stream and lay down on his blanket. He looked up at the night sky. The stars seemed so close. He wondered just how many were out there. He closed his eyes and thanked the Great Spirit for the happiness he felt. His mind filled with thoughts of the ponies. He asked the Great Spirit to help him find the right pony to share in his search for the golden light.

Quiet One was awake before the sun was up, and he started to plant the corn. He had all of his planted before Princess Windsong called him for his morning meal. He ate very fast and then went to help others plant. He worked hard for many long hours, but he always had a smile on his face, and he didn't try to rush anyone. The sun had come up seven times before finally the last kernel of corn was in the warm earth. Quiet One went to his teepee and sat down. He was tired, but he also was pleased because the planting was finished and soon he would find his pony.

The Wild Ponies

While they were eating their meal that evening, Strong Eagle told Quiet One that there was going to be a meeting in Chief Wise Owl's teepee later that evening to discuss the plan to catch the wild ponies.

"When do we leave to find the ponies, Father?"

"Tomorrow when the sun rises," answered Strong Eagle.

Quiet One grinned from ear to ear. After they finished their meal, Quiet One and his father went to the meeting. All the brothers were there, and Quiet One could feel the excitement in the air. The wild ponies had been seen grazing in a large meadow about one day's journey from the camp. They needed to drive the ponies up a small canyon. On one side of the canyon was a high rocky mountain and on the other side was a cliff. It was a box canyon, which meant it had no opening at the other end. The plan was to have the Indian brothers drive the wild ponies into this box canyon and then line up their ponies side by side to close off the entrance. Of the Indians who needed ponies, one brother at a time would enter the herd and catch his own pony.

Chief Wise Owl stood and raised his hand. Everyone became very still. Wise Owl said, "Quiet One, come here!"

Quiet One was puzzled but quickly jumped to his feet and stood before the chief, never giving any sign that this great man was also his own grandfather. Chief Wise Owl put his hands on Quiet One's shoulders and said, "We have watched you grow into a young brave whose love for all our people is so great that it makes our hearts happy. We have never known such a brother. In appreciation for your love and the hard work you so unselfishly give to us, we are proud to present you with these gifts."

One brother stood and handed the chief a beautiful blanket in different shades of blue. "This is for you to put on your pony's back."

Another brother stood and gave the chief a long braided rawhide rope. "This is to catch your pony." The chief laid the rope on top of the blanket Quiet One was holding in his outstretched arms.

A third brother gave the chief a short braided rawhide rope. "And this is to guide your pony when you are riding him."

Quiet One stood speechless. Wise Owl raised his hand again and said, "I ask the Great Spirit to guide you to your pony. I ask the Great Spirit to lead you to the golden light, to find another way to cross the great mountains."

Quiet One thanked the chief, then turned and thanked the rest of the brothers. With his wonderful gifts in his arms, he took his place beside his father. Impressed by the chief's words, he realized even more the importance of his quest.

The sun was up when Strong Eagle and his son joined the rest of the brothers at the edge of the forest. Strong Eagle was riding his spotted pony with Quiet One riding behind. Quiet One had his rawhide ropes rolled in the blue blanket and tied over his shoulder. All the Indian brothers were whooping and howling and racing each other. Quiet One held on tightly to his father's strong back as the ponies took off. He so loved this wonderful day!

The sun was in the middle of the sky when they reached the top of the mountain where they stopped their ponies and looked down onto a wide green meadow. There, grazing on spring grass, was the herd of ponies. Hundreds of them! Quiet One's heart leaped to his throat! There were so many — spotted ones, black ones, brown ones, white ones, and red ones! How could he pick his pony when they were all so beautiful?

Just as he had that thought, he saw a pony at the edge of the herd, and his heart started pounding in his chest. That was to be his pony! The pony's color was red like the setting sun, deep red, shiny, and bright. Quiet One smiled and sent love vibrations to the beautiful animal. It raised its head and looked in Quiet One's direction. He knew the pony could not see him because they were back in the trees, but he knew the pony felt his love.

The Indians rode down the small hill as slowly and quietly as they could to get in back of the herd. They reached the meadow and slowly made a half circle behind the wild ponies. Strong Eagle raised his arm high in the air and gave the signal to stampede the ponies. With loud, high, howling yells, all the brothers took off as fast as their ponies could run. The herd of wild ones threw up their heads, whirled around, and took off as fast as they could run, too. They headed for the canyon, just as planned.

Tears were streaming down Quiet One's cheeks from the wind in his face as the spotted pony ran faster and faster. He pushed his face against his father's back and laughed out loud.

Finally, the yelling and the thunder from the ponies' hooves stopped. Quiet One jumped down from the pony, as did Strong Eagle and the rest of the brothers. They quickly made a straight line with their ponies. With their rawhide ropes tied together, they had a long rope to stop the herd from passing through. The wild ponies were running back and forth, rearing, bucking, and kicking, trying to get away however they could. The brothers just stood still and did not try to approach them. They waited until the herd calmed down and were not so frightened of the trap they were in.

One by one, each brother entered the herd and caught one of the wild ponies. The pony would rear up, fighting the rawhide ropes around its neck. Some ponies would run and drag the brother at the end of the rope. Everyone was catching a pony.

Quiet One's heart nearly stopped when he saw a brother going for the red pony. But it was a very clever pony, and not one brother could get a rawhide rope near it. The red pony ran from the side of the mountain to the edge of the cliff. It stopped there and looked to the other side of the gorge. Quiet One knew the red pony was thinking that it wanted to jump to the other side, but the gorge was almost three times the length of its body.

Quiet One noticed a group of about six brothers talking and pointing to the red pony. They all started toward the pony, but it saw them coming, reared up on its hind legs, whirled around, and trotted to the side of the mountain. It turned, stood still for a moment, then lowered its head and took off on a dead run toward the cliff. Quiet One's heart was pounding as the red pony made a great leap. As it was flying across the gorge, its mane and tail looked like flaming wings that lifted it to the safety of the other side. When the pony landed, it kicked its heels in the air and disappeared into the forest.

All the brothers were left standing with their mouths wide open and their empty rawhide ropes in their hands. Quiet One jumped with joy! Strong Eagle looked at his son.

"Oh, Father! That is the pony I want!" he cried.

Strong Eagle smiled and said, "Go find it, then."

Quiet One took off running down the canyon to the meadow where he could cross to the other side of the mountain. Then he followed the gorge back up the opposite

side until he came to the place where the red pony had jumped across.

Strong Eagle came to the edge of the cliff and yelled, "I'll wait for you in the meadow." Quiet One could hardly hear his father because the other brothers were still trying to catch ponies, so he just raised his arm and so did his father. They smiled at each other, and then Quiet One also disappeared into the forest.

The red pony's hoof prints were easy to follow. Quiet One could tell that it was still running and jumping, and he knew how happy it felt after making that wonderful jump. He followed the tracks until dark when, unable to see, he decided to rest until morning. He found some sweet berries and went to the nearby stream and speared a fish. Rubbing two sticks together, he made a fire, cooked his fish, and ate the berries.

After he finished eating, he went to the stream and washed his face and hands. The cool water felt good. He was tired, but it was a good tired. He had had a wonderful day! He lay on his back in the tall grass with his blue blanket under his head for a pillow. When he closed his eyes, he could still see the red pony flying through the air with its mane and tail looking like wings. That's it! That's what I'll name my pony — Red Wings! With the vision of Red Wings in his mind, Quiet One thanked the Great Spirit and fell asleep.

Red Wings

The sun's rays peeking through the trees awakened Quiet One as they flickered in his face. He went to the fire and kicked dirt on the warm coals, then started again on the trail of Red Wings' hoof prints. He found a place where the grass was smashed flat from the weight of the pony and knew it had slept there.

Further up the trail, Quiet One came to a patch of berries and stopped to pick some. He knelt down to get the ones on the lower part of the bush, and as he pushed the bush to one side, he saw two hooves! The berries fell from his hand, and he looked up. There was Red Wings! Quiet One stood up slowly and just looked at the beautiful pony. Red Wings shook his head, snorted, and pawed the ground.

"Oh, Red Wings, you are so magnificent!" Quiet One spoke aloud but very softly. Red Wings lowered his head to Quiet One's shoulder and nibbled at the blue blanket.

"That is your blanket, and it will look beautiful on your back," Quiet One murmured as he reached out his hand to Red Wings. The red pony sniffed his hand. Then Quiet One scratched Red Wings' chin and patted the side of his head. Red Wings could feel the love from Quiet One and had no fear of him. Quiet One walked all around the pony, petting and talking to him very gently. He took the rolled blanket off his shoulder and knelt down. Red Wings lowered his head and sniffed the blanket. When Quiet One unrolled it and Red Wings smelled the rawhide ropes inside, his head jerked up.

Quiet One reached up and scratched Red Wings' forehead. "Don't worry. These ropes will never hurt you," he said and let the pony sniff the ropes all he wanted. Very loosely, he tied the rawhide rope around the pony's neck and looped it over his nose. Red Wings just shook his head and looked at Quiet One. Already they trusted each other completely.

Quiet One first put the blue blanket on Red Wings' back, then he jumped on, too, and Red Wings took off running through the forest, leaping over the bushes and fallen trees. They both enjoyed the ride. Quiet One felt like they were glued together.

After a while, he pulled Red Wings to a stop, leaned over on his neck, and gave his wonderful pony a hug. Then he turned Red Wings around and went down the mountain to the meadow to meet Strong Eagle who saw them coming and smiled. When Quiet One rode up to his father, he was so proud of Red Wings that he beamed all over.

"I named him Red Wings, Father, because he flew over the gorge! Isn't he beautiful?"

Strong Eagle nodded his head and circled around Red Wings, looking at him from every angle. "Yes, he is, my son. You have done very well. Now let us go and show your mother your pony." They raced across the meadow, each on his own pony.

Everyone came running out to meet Quiet One and Strong Eagle. The brothers had told the rest of the village about the red pony and were very happy for Quiet One. He rode

Red Wings over to show the pony to Grandfather Wise Owl and Princess Windsong.

"Isn't he beautiful, Mother?" Quiet One asked.

Princess Windsong stroked Red Wings' neck and said, "He is the most beautiful pony I have ever seen!"

Grandfather said, "I will put your ponies away for you. You both must be hungry. Go eat your meal. When you finish, I would like my grandson to come to my teepee and tell me all about the red pony."

While they were eating, Quiet One told his mother about his wonderful adventure. Then he went to his grandfather and told him. Wise Owl listened with delight.

"This red pony, does he talk to you like the deer and the butterfly?"

"Oh, yes, Grandfather, but it is different now. We talk to each other without words. I know what Red Wings is thinking and he knows what I am thinking, too," Quiet One answered.

"That's good," said Grandfather. "All of life is like that, if you listen with your inner ear. Now, tell me, what are your plans?"

"I must search for the golden light and another way for our people to cross the great mountains," Quiet One said.

"Yes," said Grandfather, "but where will you start?"

Quiet One was silent for a moment, then he said, "I will ask the Great Spirit."

Grandfather nodded gently and smiled. Quiet One hugged his grandfather and left to say goodnight to Red Wings.

He walked to the corrals where all the ponies were kept at night. Red Wings got very excited when he saw Quiet One. He didn't want to stay in the corral with the rest of the ponies. He wanted to be with Quiet One, and Quiet One knew it.

"All right," said Quiet One. He let the pole down and Red Wings stepped over. Then Quiet One put it back up. Red Wings followed him without a rope. Quiet One knew Red Wings would never leave him. They walked to the edge of the forest and they both lay down.

Quiet One closed his eyes and thanked the Great Spirit for his pony. He asked where he should start looking for the golden light, and he listened very hard. The Great Spirit showed him the stream that ran between the two high mountains just below Killem Point.

"That must be the way," he thought as he fell asleep.

The Search

At daybreak, Quiet One went to his teepee and told his mother and father what the Great Spirit had shown him.

"I must go now," he said as he gave them each a hug. He picked up his blue blanket and the rawhide ropes and left.

Grandfather was standing outside his teepee as Quiet One rode Red Wings out of the village. Quiet One stopped at his grandfather's side.

"I saw the stream that runs through the two high mountains just below Killem Point," said Quiet One.

Grandfather grasped Quiet One's hand and said, "May the Great Spirit be with you."

They looked at one another for a long moment. Then Quiet One galloped away on Red Wings.

Quiet One decided to follow the creek bottom starting at the edge of his village. This turned out to be very difficult. The water was cold and deep because it came from melted snow from the mountain peaks. It rushed down the steep mountain with a roar. Its banks were covered with brush, mostly wild rose bushes, with thorns which tore at Quiet

One's arms and legs. Fallen logs criss-crossed the creek, making it very difficult for Red Wings to jump over them. Many times the brush, fallen dead logs, and huge rocks made following one side of the creek impossible, so they had to cross over the swift, cold water to the other side. Following this creek was hard and tiring, but they kept on its path. Quiet One stopped often and let his pony rest, but he himself could not rest. His eyes were always searching for the golden light.

The sun had come up and gone down many times, and Quiet One's arms, legs, and face were bleeding from the thorn bushes and low branches of the trees, but he kept going. Soon, the brush and the trees disappeared. The stream grew wider and the rocks turned into boulders. Traveling became easier, and Quiet One relaxed and enjoyed the beautiful surroundings. But, the peaceful feeling didn't last long. The creek started rushing down the mountain, and the trail disappeared in the wild water. Soon Quiet One knew why. The creek dropped over a cliff and became a waterfall.

Quiet One looked down at the waterfall, then looked up at the high cliffs. He couldn't go down and he couldn't go up. He looked all around for the golden light, but he saw nothing. He had to go back.

Instead of following the stream again, he went up the side of the mountain, just high enough to get away from the underbrush but close enough to keep the stream in sight all the time. The Great Spirit had shown him the stream for a reason, and he wasn't about to give up. Quiet One was so thankful for Red Wings' strength as they went up and down the mountain many times. He knew he could never have traveled the mountain without his strong pony.

More days passed, and still Quiet One did not find the golden light. Both he and Red Wings were tired and sore. They crossed the stream again and went up the other side of the mountain. They went up and down and up and down, but saw nothing. At the end of another exhausting day, Quiet One lay on the bank and looked at the setting sun. He relaxed, and with the warm wind blowing on his aching body, he listened to the wind's song:

Feel the Great Spirit in the wind,
And breathe his breath as one.
Drift with the wind into the mellow light,
And enter the morning and evening sun.

He was looking at the cliffs at Killem Point. He had never seen Killem Point from this angle before, but there it was. The sun dropped behind the mountain and just below the tree line he saw a bright glow. He knew it wasn't the sun. It grew bigger and bigger! Brighter and brighter! Quiet One sat up as the bright glow turned into a brilliant golden light. Then it grew dimmer and dimmer and was gone. Quiet One knew he had finally seen his golden light, and he thanked the Great Spirit for directing his search. He slept very well that night.

The Golden Light

Quiet One was awakened by rain drops splashing on his face. He looked up at Rattlesnake Pass. Heavy rain clouds were hanging over Killem Point, and the drizzling rain made it very hard to see anything. He threw the blue blanket on Red Wings and jumped on his back. They followed the stream almost all the way back to their village. The rain was coming down much harder, and Quiet One was cold and hungry.

They crossed the stream and started up the lower end of Rattlesnake Pass. Quiet One paused for a moment to give Red Wings a short rest. He turned and looked down at his village. The smoke was curling up from the teepees, and Quiet One could almost smell his mother's morning meal. How good a hot meal would taste, and how good a warm fire would feel! He looked longingly at the little village but turned around and continued up Rattlesnake Pass. He couldn't stop now. He must find the golden light before summer was over.

They left the trail and went high up the mountain. The rain came down harder and harder, and the climb was very slow and slick. Small streams of water were running off the mountain, and Red Wings was slipping and falling to his knees.

Quiet One got off and led Red Wings through the heavy rain toward the cliffs. When they got to the cliffs, there was a small cave, and he led his pony in. There was just enough room for both of them to get out of the rain. Red Wings had steam coming off his body from the steep climb, so Quiet One took the wet blue blanket and rubbed him down. Then he looked around to see if he could find some wood or weeds for a fire, but everything was soaking wet.

Quiet One sat on a rock and watched the rain. Red Wings nibbled at his hair. Quiet One rubbed Red Wings' nose and told him they would be dry soon, and then they wouldn't be so cold. They both looked out at the heavy rain falling and felt very thankful they had found this hole in the mountain for shelter.

Rainwater started pouring off the ledge above their heads like a waterfall, then ran like a river down the mountain. They waited and waited for the rain to stop, but it kept coming down harder and harder. The lightning flashed, and the thunder roared. Quiet One became very tired, and he couldn't watch the rain any more. He asked Red Wings to lie down so he could lean against his big warm body. Then he laid his head on Red Wings' shoulder and drifted off to sleep.

A loud thunder clap brought Quiet One and Red Wings both to their feet! The waterfall above their heads had turned into mud with rocks, bushes, and branches of trees shooting off the cliff and pounding down the mountain. Quiet One couldn't believe his eyes! He sat down again and said, "Oh, Red Wings, I wish this rain would stop! I am very hungry, and I know you are, too!" Red Wings tossed his head in agreement.

At last the rain stopped, and the muddy waterfall above their heads slowed to a trickle. Quiet One stepped outside and looked at the sky. The dark rain clouds were breaking up, and there were patches of blue.

"Come on, Red Wings! Let's go find something to eat!" Quiet One exclaimed.

The rainstorm had washed away much of the earth around the roots Quiet One liked to eat. He knelt down and pulled the roots from the wet earth and cleaned them in the wet grass. Quiet One couldn't remember anything tasting so good, and he ate until his stomach was full. He waited for Red Wings to eat his fill, too. While he was watching Red Wings eat, he looked up and saw a beautiful rainbow that arched from one side of the mountain all the way over to the mountains on the opposite side.

"Red Wings, look at the rainbow! That's a sign from the Great Spirit! This will be a good day!" Quiet One announced with excitement.

The rainbow disappeared as the rain clouds lifted, and the warm sun started to shine. Oh, how good the sun felt on their chilled bodies as they traveled across the mountain. Quiet One looked down and knew they were almost directly above Killem Point. He started up the mountain toward the place where he had seen the golden light. The mountain was very steep, so Red Wings had to climb in a zig-zag pattern. When they reached the tree line just a little way from the top, Quiet One stopped and looked all around. The sun was just starting to go down. Quiet One's heart was beating fast. Everything was so silent. Then he saw it — a small glow through the trees.

"Let's go, Red Wings!"

They took off as fast as Red Wings could run. As they approached the end of the canyon, the glow turned into the brilliant golden light. There it was! There were pine trees on both sides and the big rock just like the Great Spirit had shown him in his mind. Red Wings flew over the bushes and the fallen logs, for they knew the golden light would not last long. When they reached the big rock, Quiet One pulled Red Wings to a stop and jumped off. He ran around the rock and beheld the most beautiful sight he had ever seen! He saw an archway with crystal-like rocks gleaming all around it.

It was like a tunnel. As he entered it, above his head and on both sides was pure golden light, a reflection of the setting sun off the crystal rocks. Quiet One walked in, turning around and around in awe, looking at the magnificent glow. His heart was beating so hard he could feel it pounding in his head. Red Wings followed Quiet One with great caution. Tears streamed down Quiet One's face. He had never known such happiness. They came out of the other end of the tunnel and looked down into a beautiful green valley. Quiet One knew he had found "The Other Way." He turned his tear-stained face up to the blue sky and said aloud, "Thank you, Great Spirit!"

Quiet One turned to look at the golden tunnel again, but it was completely dark. He looked for the sun, but it was gone, too. He realized that the reason no one had ever been able to find the tunnel before was because the sun entered the tunnel for only a few minutes each day at sunset. He put his arms around Red Wings' neck and said, "Thank you, my best friend! I never would have been able to find the golden light and the other way without you!"

The Other Way

The next day, Quiet One was up with the sun and went back into the tunnel, leading Red Wings behind him. It was so dark he couldn't see his hand in front of his face, so he went very slowly through the tunnel, feeling his way along the sides. Finally, he could see the light at the other end and walked a little faster. When they came out the other end, Quiet One made a mark on the big rock. Then all the way down to Rattlesnake Pass he left a trail by marking the trees. When they reached the trail leading to the start of the pass, he piled up a small mound of rocks. This would mark the trail up the mountain.

When they rode into the village, Quiet One noticed that the corn he had planted was ready to pick. His search had taken all summer.

Princess Windsong was carrying water from the stream when she saw Quiet One and Red Wings. She dropped her pots and started running toward them calling, "He's back! He's back!"

Quiet One slid off Red Wings, threw his arms around his mother and just held her tight. She pushed him away from her and wiped the tears from her face. She gently touched the cuts and scratches on his face and arms.

Strong Eagle came running to them and held Quiet One in his arms. "I am very glad you are home, my son!" he said.

Quiet One was so happy to be with his parents that he almost forgot to tell them the good news. He stepped back and shouted, "I found it! I found the other way for our people to cross the great mountains!"

Both their mouths dropped open.

"It was just like the Great Spirit had shown me — the brilliant golden light, the pine trees, the rock, everything! Our people will never have to cross Rattlesnake Pass and Killem Point again!"

Strong Eagle said, "My son, we could never go over Rattlesnake Pass again. The great rainstorm completely washed away Killem Point. The lightning bolts split the cliffs and the whole side of the mountain gave way."

Now Quiet One's mouth dropped open!

When Quiet One was called to the teepee of Chief Wise Owl, all the Indian brothers were there. The chief asked him to tell about his long search for the golden light and the other way. When Quiet One had finished telling everything, Chief Wise Owl stood and said, "We will have a celebration tonight to thank the Great Spirit for sending our brave young brother, Quiet One, home to us. Then, with the morning sun, we will follow our brother to the golden light."

When the sun was up, so was all the village. Everyone felt great joy and excitement. There was love and thankfulness in Quiet One's heart as he led them up the mountain. The trail was easy to follow and they made it to the top a long time before the sun was ready to set. Grandfather Wise Owl, Princess Windsong, and Strong Eagle could hardly wait for the wonderful moment. As the sun was going down, everyone gathered around the entrance to the tunnel. Slowly the glow was seen through the opening.

Quiet One took his mother's hand and led her through the archway. The others followed. As before, the tunnel was lit with the brilliance of the sun's reflection off the crystal rocks. When they reached the other end of the tunnel and looked into the beautiful valley below, there were shouts of joy! There was crying and hugging! There was dancing, and there were many who were just silent.

Grandfather put his arm around Quiet One's shoulder and said, "I am so proud of you, my grandson. I thank the Great Spirit for sending you to us, not only for finding the other way, but for reminding us of what we can do if we open our hearts and minds to the Great Spirit."

On the large rock in front of the golden tunnel, Strong Eagle wrote these words:

As you pass through this golden light
And journey on your way,
Remember my son, Quiet One, and
What he had to say.
Take the time to stop, to look,
And to listen.
For you have passed the Great Spirit God
One hundred times today.